Published 1986 by Derrydale Books,
distributed by Crown Publishers, Inc.

Produced for Derrydale Books by
Victoria House Publishing Ltd.
4/5 Lower Borough Walls
Bath BA1 1QR, England

Copyright © 1986 Victoria House Publishing Ltd

Printed in Singapore

Teddy
Gets Lost

Illustrated by Stephen Cartwright
Written by Jean Kenward

Derrydale Books
New York

Today, we are going out shopping.
Teddy is coming, too.

Bump! We go off the curb and across the street. We meet Mommy's friend.

This is the drug store. Mommy buys some
bottles. We put them in the basket.

But where is Teddy? We don't have him
anymore. We can't see him anywhere.

Is he outside, in the road? We look both
ways. Up and down. No, he is not there.

Am I sitting on him? Mommy lifts me up.
There is a scarf and a carrot—but not Teddy.

We go on with our shopping without Teddy.

We buy some pears, some bananas, and some red apples. Mommy gives me an apple to bite.

We buy some ice cream. It is cold!

"We have lost Teddy," Mommy says
to the man at the fish counter.
He is sorry. So am I!

When we go home we go past the Toy Shop.

There are teddies in the window—big ones,
and little ones. But not MY teddy.

Bump! We go off the curb again and across the street. "Hi! Hi!" calls a voice.

It is Mommy's friend. She runs after us.
She is holding Teddy!

"You left Teddy behind when we were talking!" she says. "Here he is!"

"Oh, thank you! I am glad!" sighs Mommy.
Teddy is FOUND! I give him a BIG HUG.